IF YOU WERE A...

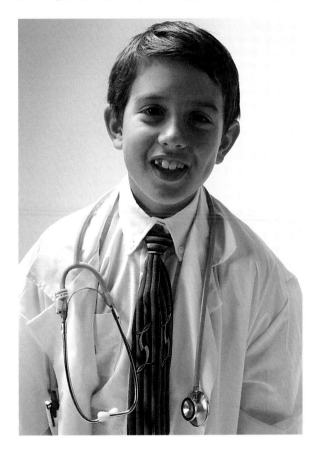

Doctor

HOWARD MILLER LIBRARY
14 S. CHURCH STREET
ZEELAND, MI 49464
1-616-772-0874

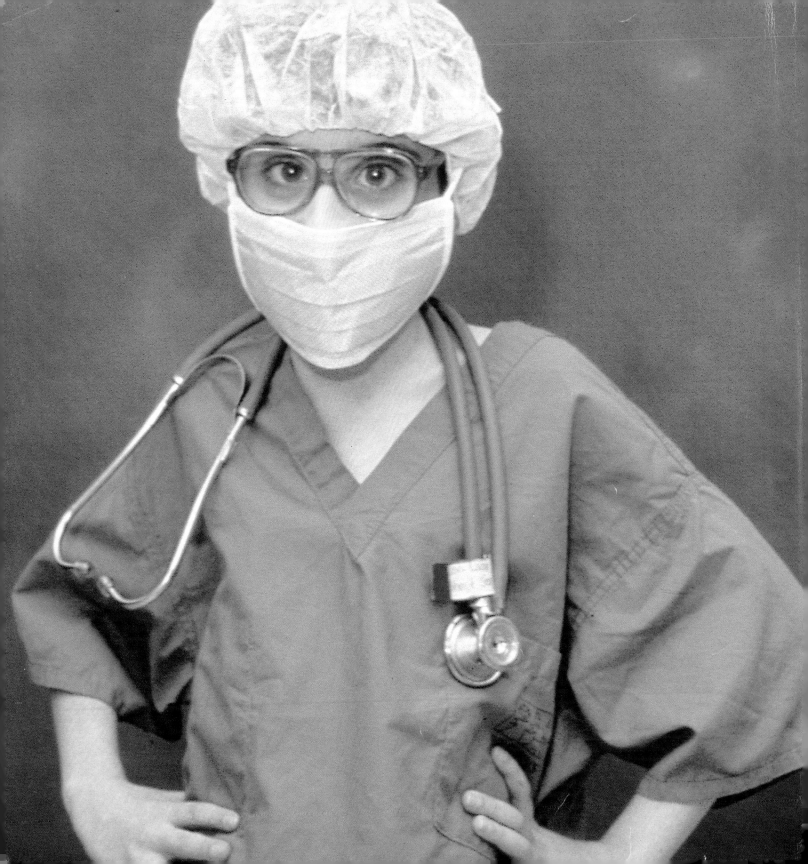

IF YOU WERE A...
Doctor

Virginia Schomp

BENCHMARK BOOKS

MARSHALL CAVENDISH
NEW YORK

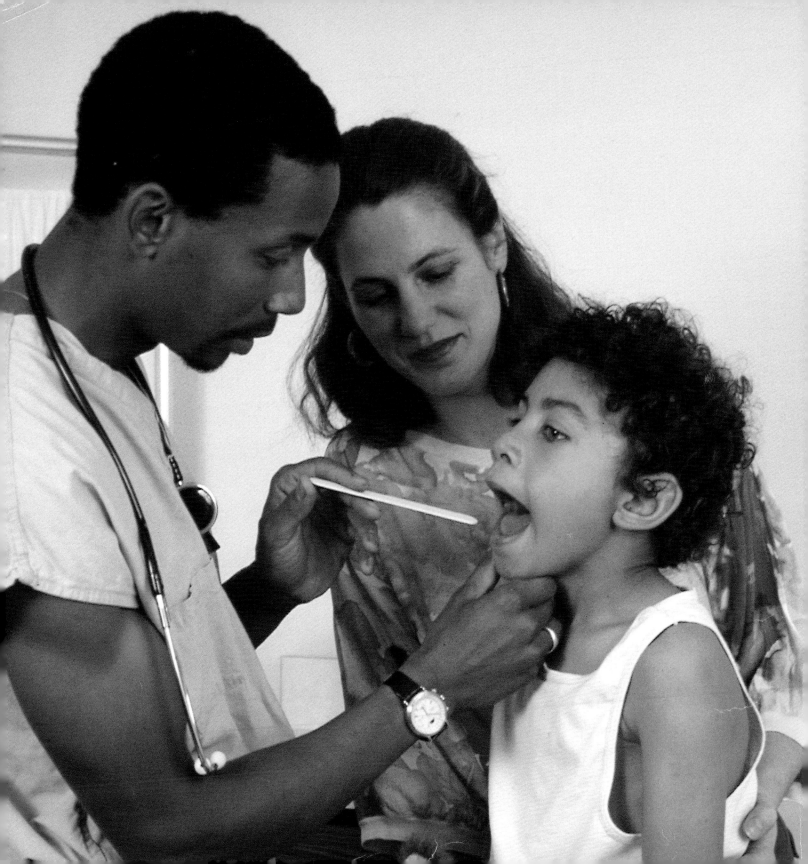

A doctor must know how to check for illness . . .

. . . and, sometimes, how to talk a patient into taking his medicine.

If you were a doctor, you would help people stay healthy and strong. When they're sick, you would help them get better.

This boy's throat is red and scratchy. You give him medicine to make him well. Next you treat a girl who sprained her ankle playing soccer.

A woman with a cough, a baby with a rash, a man who needs an operation to make his heart stronger— you'd never know who might need your help next if you were a doctor.

The doctor's day starts early. While the world is just waking, many doctors are already at the hospital, doing "rounds." Walking from room to room, they visit their patients to make sure each is getting well.

Notes help the doctor keep track of a patient's health, so he'll know when she's ready to go home.

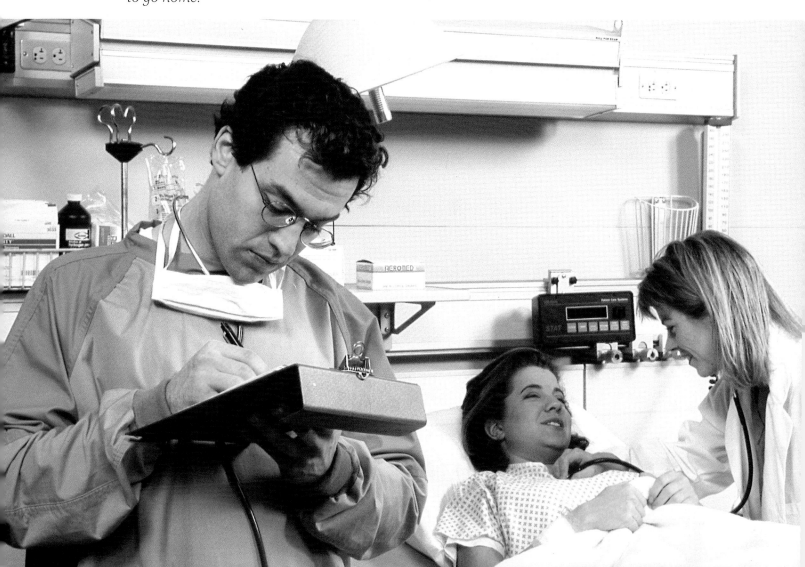

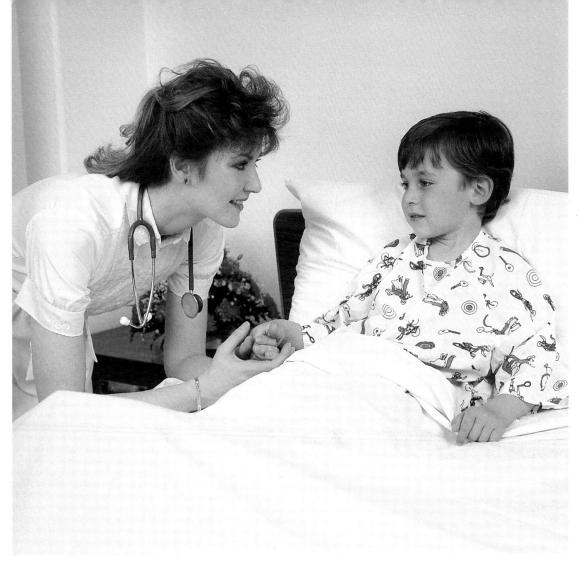

Nurses help the doctor make sure patients feel safe and comfortable.

Many of the doctors are family physicians (fuh-ZIH-shuns). Their patients include boys and girls, moms and dads, grandmas and grandpas. Family physicians take care of all kinds of people with all kinds of problems.

Sometimes sharing a laugh is the best medicine.

It's nine o'clock. Rounds are done. But more people are waiting in the family physician's office. "How are you today?" the doctor asks each patient. Asking questions and really listening to the answers is one good way to find out why a person may be feeling sick.

If you were a family physician, you would also use special tools to look and listen inside the body. *Thump-thump. Whoosh.* A stethoscope (STETH-uh-scope) helps you tune in to the sounds of a patient's heartbeat and breathing.

Using a stethoscope, the doctor listens to sounds in the body.

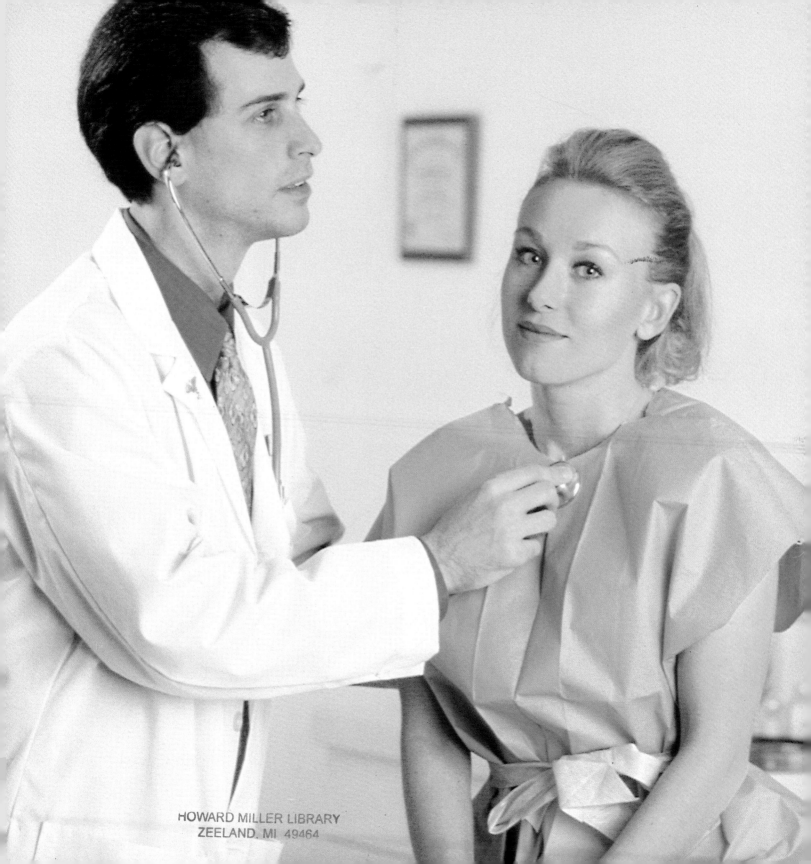

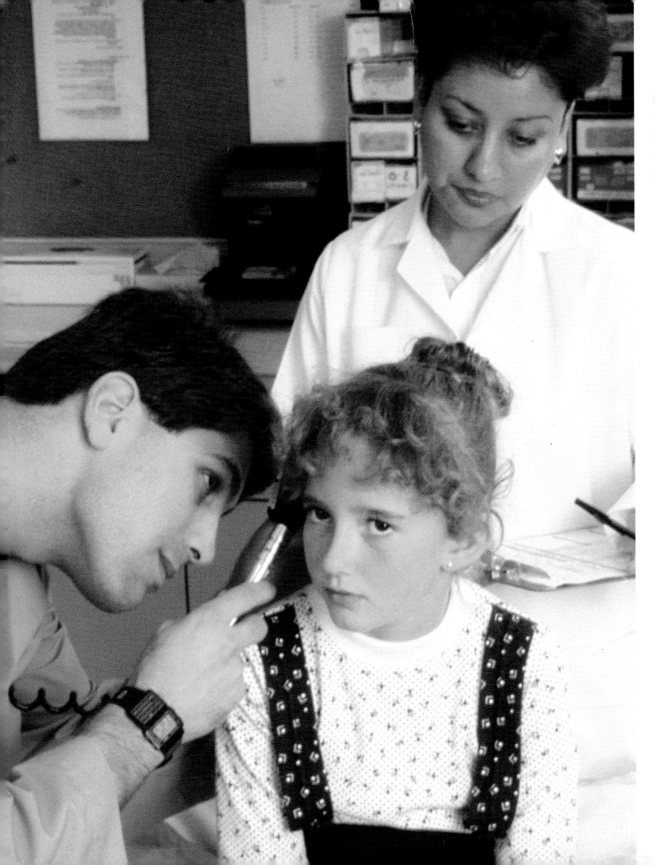

An otoscope (OH-tuh-scope) lets the doctor check for infection in the ears.

An otoscope has a tiny light for looking inside ears. Other tools help you check eyes, nose, and throat. There are even tools for measuring how hard a person's heart is working.

By listening and looking, you've figured out what's wrong. Now, what will you do about it? Maybe you'll write a prescription—an order to the drugstore for medicine to make the patient well. You might talk about the foods, exercise, and rest everyone needs to stay healthy.

An ophthalmoscope (ahf-THAL-muh-scope) is used to inspect the inside of the eye.

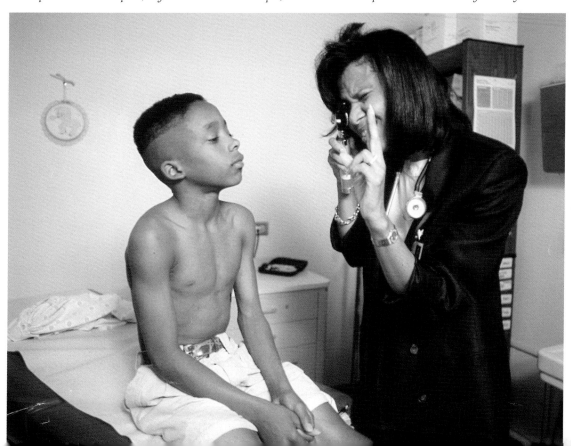

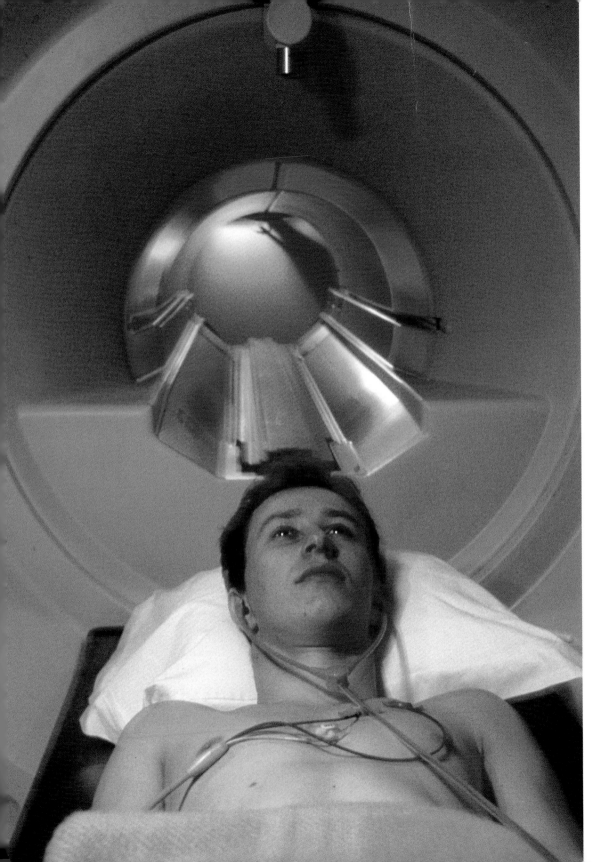

An MRI machine uses radio waves to take pictures of the brain and other parts of the body.

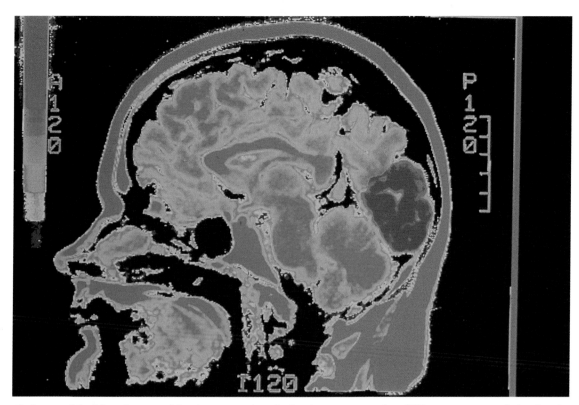

Colors added by the machine's computer help doctors see the different parts of the brain.

Sometimes it's hard to tell what is making someone sick. The doctor must send a small amount of the patient's blood to the laboratory. Tests done in the lab unlock the secret of what's going on inside the patient's body.

For an even closer look inside, doctors use amazing machines that take pictures right through the skin. The pictures can show a football player's broken bone or the ring swallowed by his pet poodle.

Five o'clock—the last patient has left the office. But the family physician's day isn't over yet.

Illness and accidents can happen anytime. At home the doctor's pager beeps again and again. Patients are calling with questions about their health and treatment.

Sometimes a call means that someone is badly hurt or ill. The doctor rushes to the hospital to help. Day and night, hospitals are busy places, filled with worried patients and the doctors and nurses who work hard to save lives.

Any time of the day or night, doctors and other trained people are ready to help at the hospital.

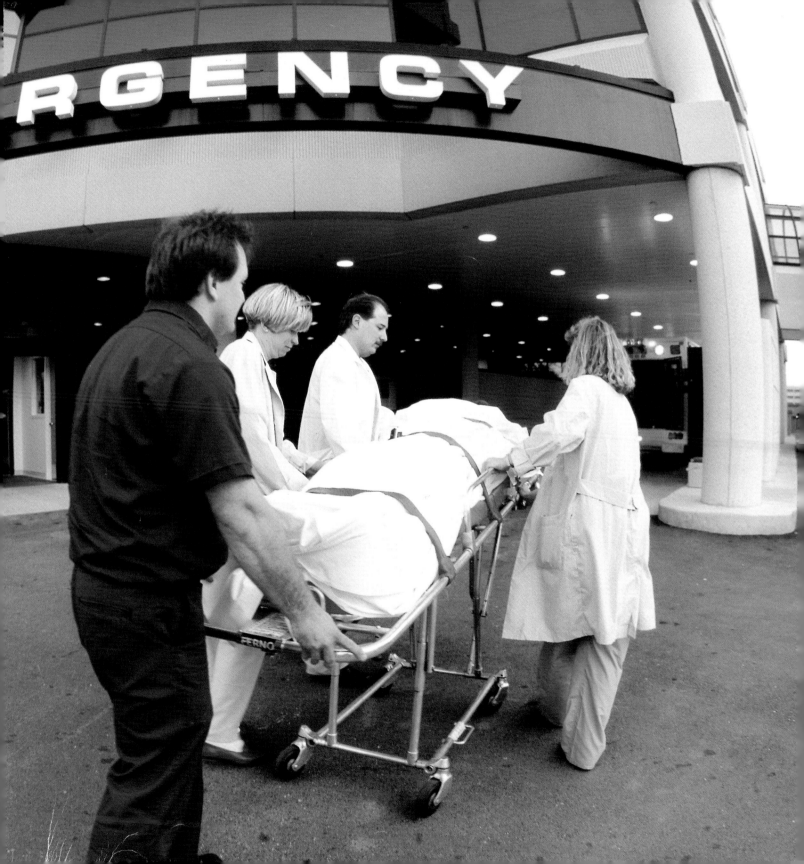

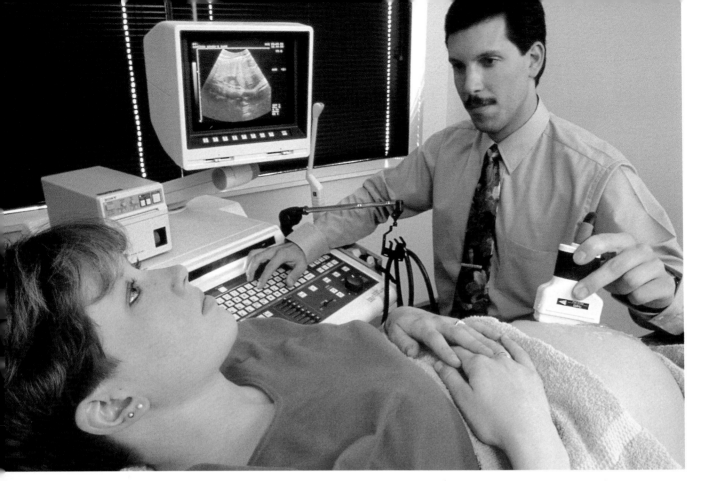

An ultrasound machine lets the doctor see the baby inside its mother's body.

Family physicians take care of all kinds of patients. But some doctors treat only certain problems or certain kinds of people.

Obstetricians (ahb-stuh-TRIH-shuns) are doctors who care for mothers-to-be. Pregnant women go to their obstetrician every month. The doctor checks that both the mother and the baby growing inside her are healthy.

At last, the big day! Giving birth is hard work, but the obstetrician makes sure mother and baby stay strong. Imagine the excitement and joy of bringing a new life into the world!

A new mother gets ready to hold her baby for the first time.

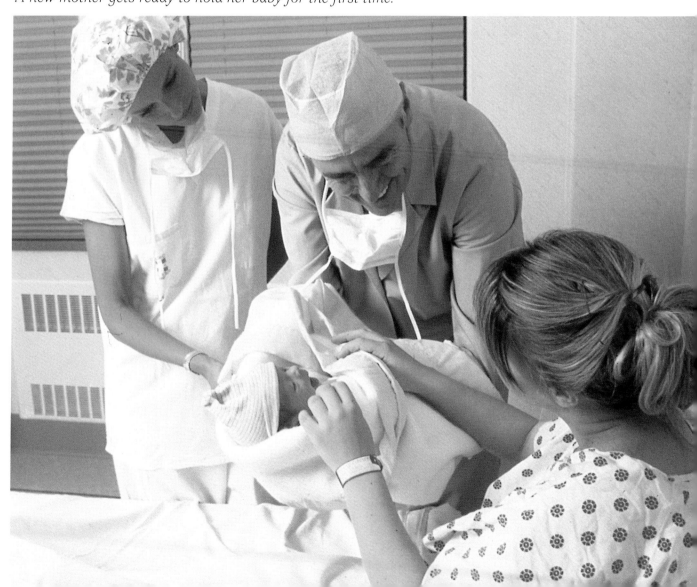

Who will take care of the new baby's health? A doctor called a pediatrician (pee-dee-uh-TRIH-shun). Pediatricians are experts in the care, growth, and illnesses of children of all ages.

Babies who get sick need the pediatrician's extra-special care.

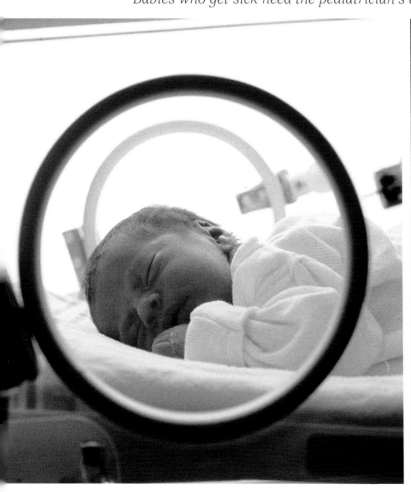 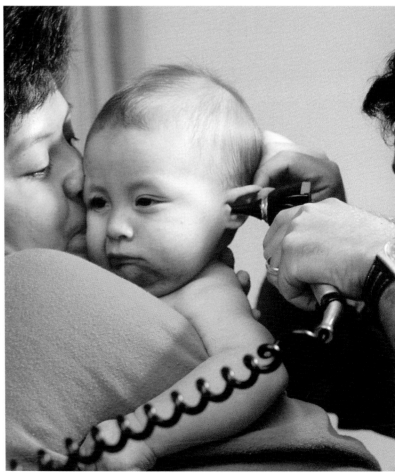

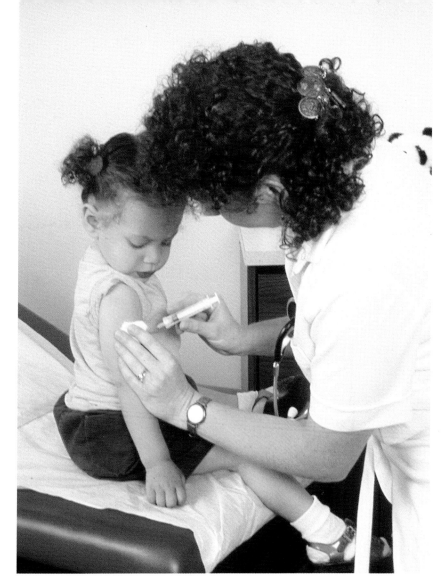

A shot of a medicine called a vaccine (vak-SEEN) will protect this girl from disease.

If you were a pediatrician, you would give children checkups to make sure their bodies are growing properly. You'd give them shots to prevent diseases. When a child has a sore throat or an upset stomach, you'd know which medicine is best at fighting the germs.

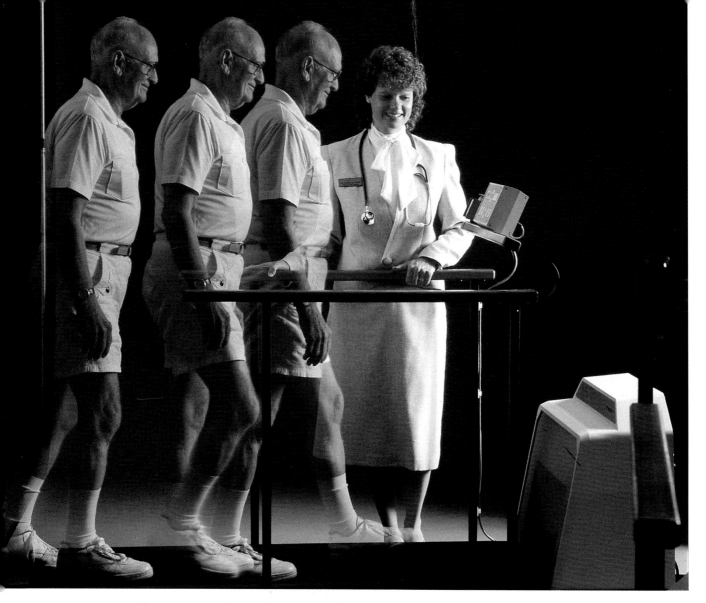

The photographer had fun with this trick shot of a man who is taking his heart doctor's advice—get up on that exercise treadmill and keep going . . . and going . . . and going . . .

Some doctors are experts in the needs and problems of older adults. Because of their special training, they can help patients live a healthy, comfortable old age.

Other doctors know all about one part of the body. There are eye doctors; skin doctors; ear, nose, and throat doctors. There are doctors who work only in hospital emergency rooms and some who work in labs, looking for new drugs to conquer diseases.

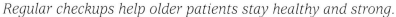

Regular checkups help older patients stay healthy and strong.

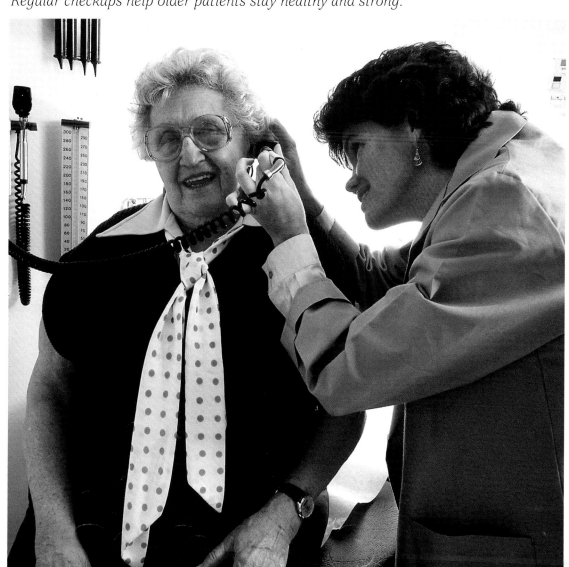

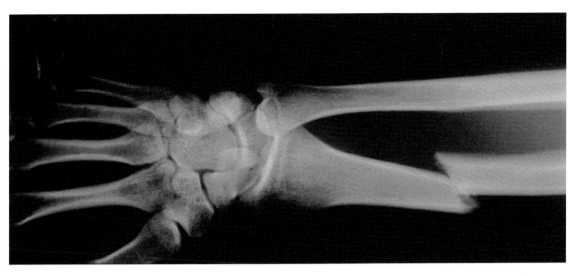

X rays showed the doctor where the arm was broken.

Orthopedists (or-thuh-PEE-dists) are doctors whose specialty is bones. This girl broke her arm in a fall from her bike. The orthopedist had X-ray pictures taken to see exactly where the bone was broken.

Broken bones heal themselves, as long as they're not moved. To keep the girl's bone in place, the orthopedist wrapped her arm in a cast. In a few weeks, the doctor will take the cast off. She'll send her patient back to her bike, with a warning—watch out for those curbs!

A cast will keep this girl's bones from moving while her broken arm heals.

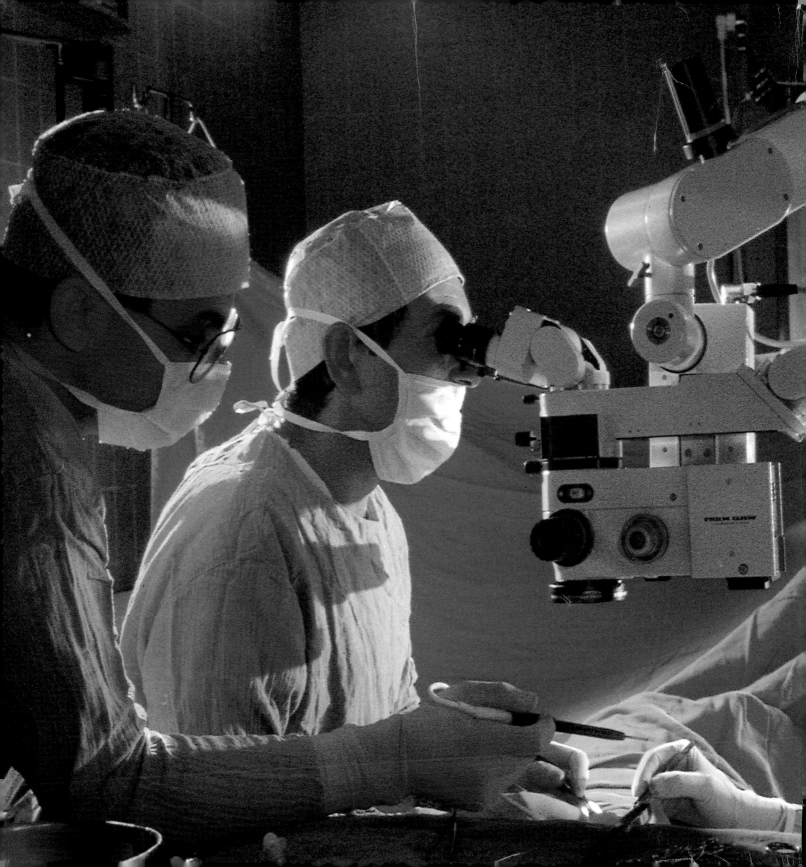

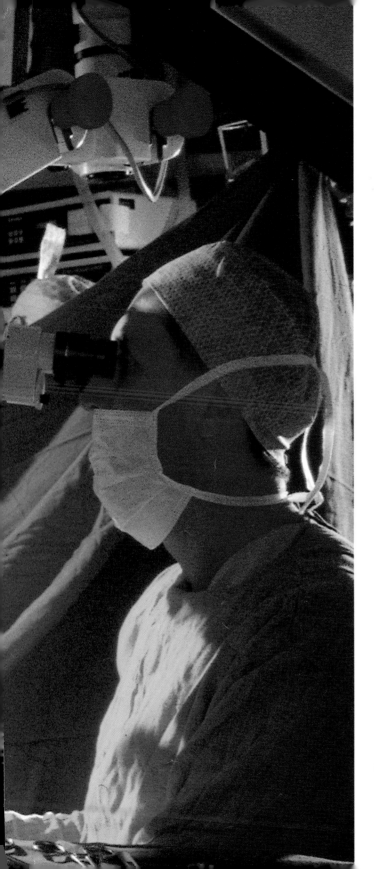

Sometimes patients can't be cured with medicine or a cast. If the trouble is serious, the doctor may have to operate. Operating means cutting the body open to work on the disease or injury.

Doctors who operate are called surgeons (SUR-jihns). They need good hands and lots of energy, because a complicated operation can last hours. Other doctors and nurses help. The room may be noisy and crowded. But thanks to the anesthetic (an-us-THET-ik)—a special drug that blocks pain—the patient stays sound asleep.

The operating room is an exciting place filled with skilled doctors and complex machinery.

Medical school students spend hours in the classroom, studying how the body works.

Do you like helping people? Are you good at thinking your way through problems? If you study and work hard, you could become a doctor.

First you must go to college and medical school. Next you'll work in a hospital as a resident, or student doctor. Altogether it takes eleven or more years of training to become a family physician, pediatrician, or other type of doctor.

Are you ready to learn how to make people well? Will you heal a hurt, save a life, bring new lives into the world?

Students also get a chance to work with experienced doctors and to share ideas and dreams with one another.

DOCTORS IN TIME

For many centuries, doctors believed that bleeding, or "blood-letting," cured illness by draining poisons from the body.

Two thousand years ago, the Greek healer Hippocrates set down rules for patient care that doctors have followed ever since.

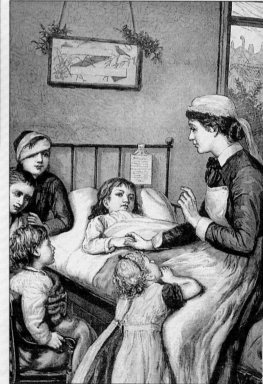

Before the 1850s, most nurses were poorly trained and hospitals were often dark and dirty. Florence Nightingale set up schools to teach nurses about the importance of cleanliness and proper patient care.

The nineteenth century was a time of great discoveries in medicine. French scientist Louis Pasteur was the first to prove that germs cause illness.

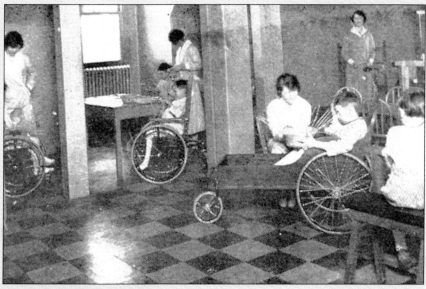

In the early 1900s, doctors found new ways to help children in hospitals get well.

Marie Curie and her husband, Pierre, discovered radium in 1898. Today this rare metal is used to treat cancer.

A DOCTOR'S CLOTHING AND INSTRUMENTS

Doctors may wear a white lab coat and scrubs—a loose-fitting shirt and pants.

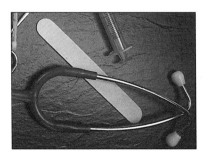

tongue depressor—for holding down the tongue so the doctor can check the throat

stethoscope (STETH-uh-scope)—for listening to heart and lungs

scalpel—knife used in operations

otoscope (OH-tuh-scope)—for checking ears

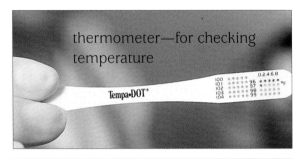

thermometer—for checking temperature

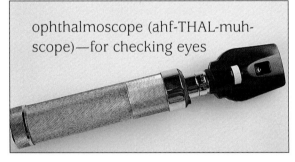

ophthalmoscope (ahf-THAL-muh-scope)—for checking eyes

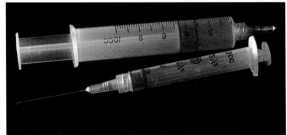

syringe (suh-RINJ)—needle for giving shots

WORDS TO KNOW

anesthetic (an-us-THET-ik) A drug given during an operation so the patient will not feel pain.

family physician (fuh-ZIH-shun) A doctor who treats patients of all ages for many different kinds of problems.

obstetrician (ahb-stuh-TRIH-shun) A doctor who treats mothers-to-be and delivers babies.

orthopedist (or-thuh-PEE-dist) A doctor who treats problems with the body's skeleton and bones.

pediatrician (pee-dee-uh-TRIH-shun) A doctor who treats only children.

prescription An order for medicine written by a doctor to the druggist.

surgeon (SUR-jihn) A doctor who performs operations.

X ray A picture of the inside of the body, taken by an X-ray machine.

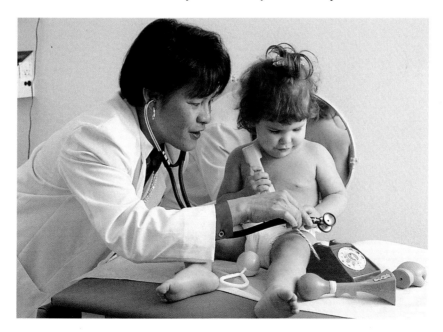

This book is for Carol,
super nurse and sister

Benchmark Books
Marshall Cavendish Corporation
99 White Plains Road
Tarrytown, New York 10591
Copyright © 2001 by Marshall Cavendish Corporation

All rights reserved. No part of this book may be reproduced or utilized in any form or by any means electronic or mechanical including photocopying, recording, or by any information storage and retrieval system, without permission from the copyright holders.

Library of Congress Cataloging-in-Publication Data
Schomp, Virginia, (date)
If you were a—doctor / Virginia Schomp
p.cm.   Includes index.
Summary: Describes in simple terms the training, education, skills, and duties of a doctor.
ISBN 0-7614-1000-7 (lib.bdg.)
1. Physicians—Training of—Juvenile literature. 2. Medicine—Vocational guidance—Juvenile literature. [1. Physicians. 2. Occupations.] I.
Title: Doctor. II. Title
R690 .S353 2000   610.69—dc21   99-086918

Photo Research by Rose Corbett Gordon, Mystic CT

Cover: *Custom Medical Stock Photo, Inc:* K. Glaser Associates

All photographs were provided by *Custom Medical Stock Photo, Inc:*
1, 7, 10, 11, 14–15, 21, 22, 23, 26, 30 (top three on right); K. Glaser Associates, 2, 8; L. Steinmark, 4, 5, 18 (right); T. McCarthy, 6, 9; BSIP, 12, 24–25; Michael Fisher, 13; Kevin Beebe, 16, 20; Keith, 17; Eric Herzog, 18 (left); G.DeGrazia, 19; Mike Moreland, 27 (left); Sean O'Brien, 27 (right); J. Fishkin, 28 (top left); EpConcepts, 28 (center), 29 (top left & top right); Historical Pictures, 28 (bottom right); Jean-Loup Charmet/SPL, 29 (bottom); Journalism Services, 30 (top left); Vincent Zuber, 30 (center top); Eric Nelson, 30 (bottom left); Pete Saloutos, 30 (bottom center); P.Stocklein, 30 (bottom right)

Printed in Hong Kong
1 3 5 7 8 6 4 2

02-3895

INDEX

education and training, 26–27

family physicians, 6–16

history of doctors, 28–29

hospitals, 6, 14, 21

medicine, 5, 11, 19

obstetricians, 16–17

orthopedists, 23

pediatricians, 18–19

surgeons, 25